Our Haunted

By Bud Simpson
Illustrated by Lloyd Birmingham

Modern Publishing
A Division of Unisystems, Inc.
New York, New York 10022
Series UPC#: 19560

Halloween was Kitty and Kent's favorite holiday. But this year they were not excited about costumes and trick-or-treating. This year, the week before Halloween was moving time, and they were not happy about it.

"Why do we have to move into this creaky old house, anyway?" Kitty grumbled.

"You know why," said Mom. "We need the space. We're lucky Aunt Clara left this house to us. We just have to fix it up a little."

"It looks haunted," Kent chimed in.

"At least Blackie the Halloween cat will like it," laughed Mom.

"I bet she won't," said Kitty.

"Why don't you get her and see?" Dad suggested.

But when Kitty found the carrying case, it was empty!

"Oh, no, we lost our Halloween cat right before Halloween!" wailed Kent. "This house is bad luck! I hate it!"

"Blackie is probably just exploring in the yard," said Mom. "She'll come in when she's hungry."

"What if she jumped out of the car when we stopped for gas?" cried Kitty. "She could be lost."

"If she doesn't turn up, she's probably still at the old house," said Dad. "We can drive back tomorrow and get her. Come on. Let's go look around."

"This is spooky," said Kitty. She had a bad feeling about the old house.

"Those sheets look like ghosts," Kent added.

"We'll leave them on till we finish moving, to protect the furniture," Mom said briskly. "Why don't you kids go up and check out your rooms?"

The children started up the winding staircase. With each step, the old stairs creaked and groaned.

"Oooh, these stairs are creepy," Kent whispered.

"They're just old," said Kitty. "Stop scaring yourself." But she secretly agreed. She marched into Kent's new room.

"Wow!" exclaimed Kitty. "Look how big your room is!" She began to feel better.

"Those big windows are scary," said Kent. "Something could come in."

"Don't be a baby," said Kitty. But she didn't feel so brave anymore. She wished Blackie were there to cuddle.

"Let's explore the attic," she said, trying not to feel scared.

They tiptoed upstairs. "It's dark up here," Kent whined. Then he screamed.

"What's the matter?" Kitty whispered.

"Something touched me."

Kitty squinted into the shadows and shuddered. "It's probably a cobweb," she said uncertainly. "Wait a minute. Your eyes will get used to the dark."

She spotted a big old trunk in a corner and pulled out an old-fashioned dress.

"Here's a cool Halloween costume," she said. "Maybe this haunted house is good for something."

She started across the room to look in an old mirror. Just then, there was a creak on the stairs. Kitty and Kent froze.

"Mom? Dad?" Kitty whispered. There was no answer, but a shadow flashed across the mirror.

"Was that you?" asked Kent.

"No," Kitty said softly. "I'm over here." At that, Kent screamed and took off down the stairs.

"Wait for me!" yelled Kitty, close behind.

The living room was empty.
"Where is everyone?" said Kitty.
Kent pointed to a big armchair. "Why is that sheet moving?"
he whispered.

"Maybe it's the wind," said Kitty. But then she looked around and her eyes got big. The windows were all closed.

The sheet moved again. "Run!" cried Kent.

The children took off through the house and into the backyard.

"Mom! Dad!" Kent shouted.

"No one's out here," said Kitty.

"Then why is that swing moving?" asked Kent, pointing.

"This time it is the wind." Kitty frowned. "But if it's the wind, why aren't all the swings moving?"

"It's the ghost!" cried Kent. "It's following us! Mom! Dad!"

Shrieking, the kids ran to the front of the house.

Mom and Dad were sitting on the porch.

"Help," sobbed Kent. "This house is haunted. We have to move!"

"Very funny," said Dad.

"No, really," gasped Kitty. "The swings were moving by themselves!"

Dad frowned. "You're just looking for reasons not to like this house."

"This is our home now," said Mom. "Let's make it feel like one. How would you like a pizza?"

Even pizza didn't taste right in that strange house.

That night there was a terrible storm. Lightning streaked the sky, and thunder boomed. Kent heard a loud banging. "Kitty!" he called. "It's after me!"

"Here I am," she said, sitting down by him. "It's just a broken shutter." She got up to close the window.

Just then a lightning bolt flashed, revealing two bright yellow eyes outside the window. A shape darted across a branch. As the children shrank back, it leaped right into Kent's room!

Kent and Kitty raced down the hall and dived into their parents' bed.

"Mom! Dad! Wake up!" screamed Kent. "Now the ghost is in my room! We have to move tonight!"

"There's no such thing as ghosts," yawned Dad.

"B-but we saw it!" Kitty stammered. "I swear!"

"Come on, I'll show you there's nothing in your room."

The children followed Dad to Kent's room.

Dad closed the window. Then he looked under the bed and in the closet. "No ghosts here," he said.

"We saw it come in the window," Kent insisted.

"We are not leaving this house," Dad said firmly. "So you can stop this nonsense. Sleep with us tonight, and we'll discuss it in the morning."

But even in their parents' room, Kitty and Kent couldn't sleep. They heard creaking and thumping overhead.

"The ghost is back in the attic," Kent sniffled. "Let's wake up Mom and Dad."

"They won't believe us." Kitty shivered. "We'll just have to take them up there tomorrow."

The next morning, they held their breath as Dad patiently searched the attic.

"You see?" he said. "There's nothing—" Suddenly he stiffened. Kent grabbed Kitty's hand as Dad shined his flashlight into an open trunk.

"I found the ghost," he said softly. "Come look."

Trembling, the kids peered into the trunk. Something moved!
"Relax," said Dad. "It's a friendly ghost." He shined the light in.
There, curled up in a bunch of old clothes, was Blackie.
"That's why we couldn't find her yesterday," said Mom.
"She was busy exploring her new home. She must have been

locked out last night and climbed up the tree to get in
the window."

"What a smart cat!" exclaimed Kent, scratching Blackie's
ears. She jumped up and ran downstairs. They followed her
to the living room.

"Look!" said Kitty. Blackie was under the sheet on the sofa.
"She's the ghost all right," said Kent.
"Mom was right," Kitty added. "She does seem at home in this Halloween house. It's a good house for a Halloween cat."
"It's a good house for a Halloween party, too," said Kent.
Mom and Dad smiled. "You can invite some of your old friends."
"And maybe some new ones, too," Kitty said hopefully.
Under the sheet, Blackie purred.